PEGGONY-PO

A Whale of a Tale

by ANDREA DAVIS PINKNEY

illustrated by BRIAN PINKNEY

 Jump at the Sun   Hyperion Books for Children/New York

Printed in Singapore

First Edition

1 3 5 7 9 10 8 6 4 2

This book is set in Pabst.

Reinforced binding

ISBN 0-7868-1958-8

Library of Congress Cataloging-in-
Publication Data on file.

Visit www.jumpatthesun.com

ACKNOWLEDGMENTS
Special thanks to the North Cape Nautical
Center, Provincetown, Massachusetts;
the Whaling Museum in Sag
Harbor, New York;
and the
Pier 17
crew of
the *Peking* and
the staff of the South
Street Seaport Museum,
New York City.

When the flicker of the northern lights shines its arc for thee,
That is when hard wanting strikes. Now, cast a wish to sea.

—*From an old sea shanty*

EVER HEARD THE STORY OF PEGGONY-PO? It's a story that begins with a whale, ends with a whale, and has a whole lot of whale in its middle.

When Peggony-Po came into this world, his pa, Galleon Keene, knew he was special. The boy was as feisty as a kettle of just-caught fish, and oh, was he ever quick. When he was still in burlap booties he could climb the lookout mast that towered over the *Windstead*, the whaling ship on which he and his father lived.

Never mind that he started out small and stayed small. Peggony-Po was brave. He didn't shy back from nobody or no thing—not even whales. By the time Peggony-Po was four years old, he'd caught himself his first whale.

But there was one whale no one could catch.

The whale's name was Cetus. That monster was sixty tons of high-grade blubber. He loved to smash boats with a single slam of his tail. And he ate anything that got in his way. Before Peggony-Po came to be, Galleon Keene had come close to catching Cetus many times. Galleon's final try was the most memorable.

"There blows!" Galleon had shouted.

He tried to spear the whale, but his harpoon bounced off the beast's flesh like a twig. That's when Cetus snapped the boat in two with his enormous teeth. Along with the boat, Cetus bit off one of Galleon's legs!

Galleon floated to safety on a hunk of driftwood. His heart was heavy from one more failed try at catching Cetus. It was heavier still from knowing that Cetus had stolen his leg—and his ability to go a-whaling.

A few nights later, something special happened. The northern lights flashed their cape across the sky, and they put a strange hankering in Galleon. Alone in his cabin, Galleon wished for a son. Someone to carry on the family trade.

Galleon considered the hunk of driftwood he'd used to float to safety. And he got an idea. "I'll *make* me a boy!"

First he carved a head, with ears, nose, and a chin. Then came the eyes, set deep in the boy's face. When he carved the child's lips, they parted right away. And the boy spoke.

"The rest of me," he said. "Bring on the rest of me."

Galleon worked and worked.

"Hurry!" shouted the boy. "I want to be!"

Galleon sanded the boy smooth, and gave him a beautiful
dark complexion with a stain made from pekoe tea.

He named his son after a sea shanty, a song of hope meant
to lift a sailor's spirits in the bleakest times.

Oh we'll capture bounty from the sea below,
   Peggony-Po, Peggony-Po!
It's a rich hit of bootle that'll keep us afloat,
   Peggony-Po, Peggony-Po!
We needn't fear the undertow!
   Peggony-Po, where it blows?
Peggony-Po! Peggony-Po! Peggony-Po! Peggony-Po!

Galleon hugged his boy close. "You're the answer to my
prayers," he told Peggony-Po.

"Without you, I wouldn't be me," Peggony-Po said to his pa.
"I got all my parts—including a heart that's filled with
thankfulness. But where goes your leg?"

Galleon told the boy all about Cetus. "Ever
since Cetus ate the limb of me," he explained,
"nobody will dare to try and capture the whale."

To that, Peggony-Po answered quick. "I
ain't nobody."

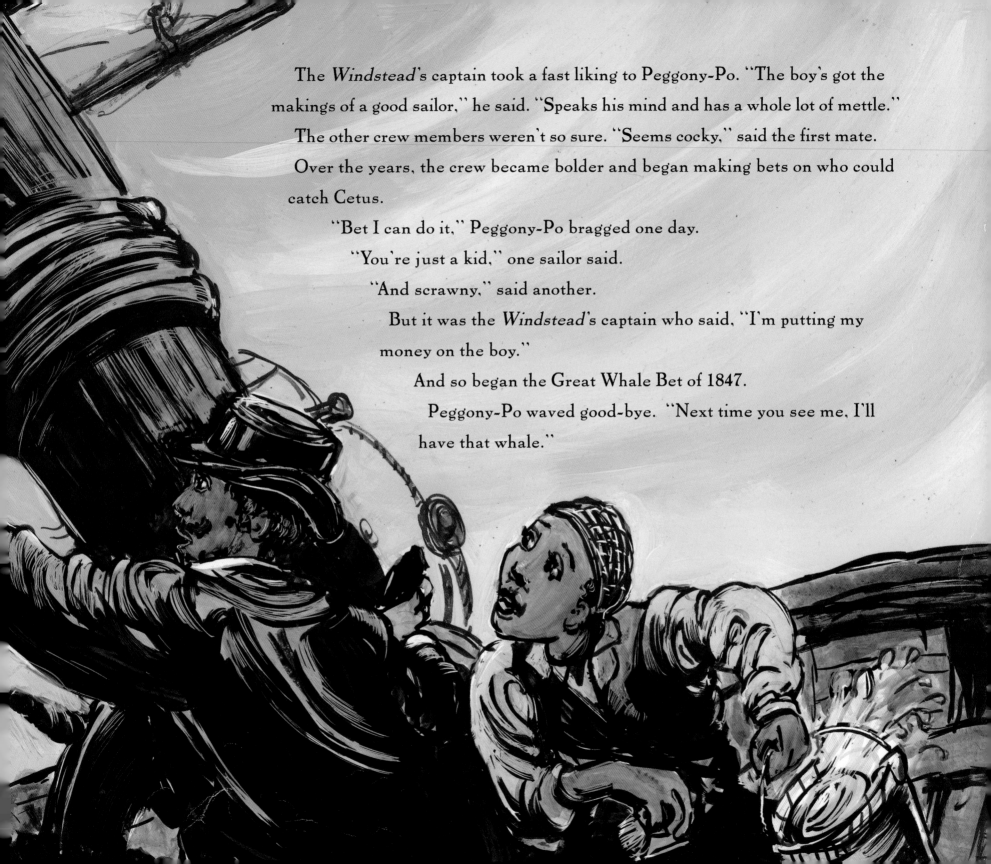

The *Windstead*'s captain took a fast liking to Peggony-Po. "The boy's got the makings of a good sailor," he said. "Speaks his mind and has a whole lot of mettle." The other crew members weren't so sure. "Seems cocky," said the first mate. Over the years, the crew became bolder and began making bets on who could catch Cetus.

"Bet I can do it," Peggony-Po bragged one day.

"You're just a kid," one sailor said.

"And scrawny," said another.

But it was the *Windstead*'s captain who said, "I'm putting my money on the boy."

And so began the Great Whale Bet of 1847.

Peggony-Po waved good-bye. "Next time you see me, I'll have that whale."

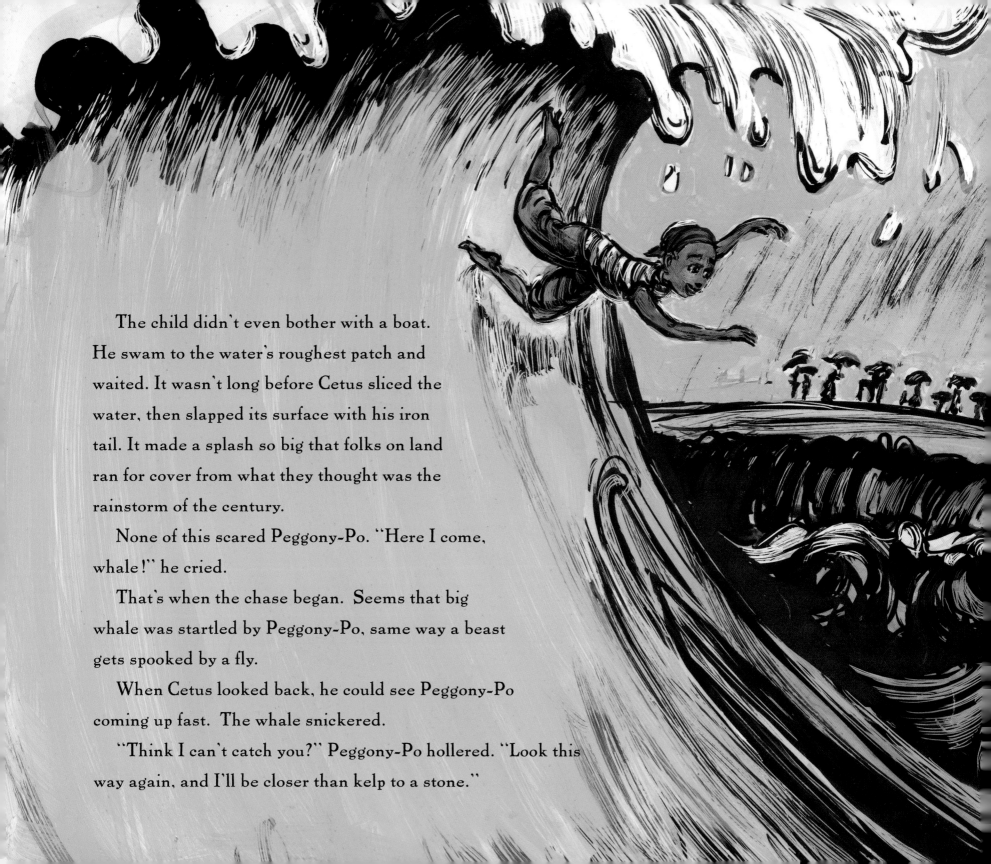

The child didn't even bother with a boat. He swam to the water's roughest patch and waited. It wasn't long before Cetus sliced the water, then slapped its surface with his iron tail. It made a splash so big that folks on land ran for cover from what they thought was the rainstorm of the century.

None of this scared Peggony-Po. "Here I come, whale!" he cried.

That's when the chase began. Seems that big whale was startled by Peggony-Po, same way a beast gets spooked by a fly.

When Cetus looked back, he could see Peggony-Po coming up fast. The whale snickered.

"Think I can't catch you?" Peggony-Po hollered. "Look this way again, and I'll be closer than kelp to a stone."

Cetus worked every ton of his blubber to escape the boy. Peggony-Po used every ounce of his wooden arms and legs to swim after the beast.

Cetus rammed through schools of fish. Peggony-Po did underwater cartwheels to keep those fish from crying. He never slowed down, though. Peggony-Po was at the whale's tail in no time.

"Get back here, Cetus!" he said. Then he swam alongside Cetus's giant eye. "Looking for lunch?" he asked.

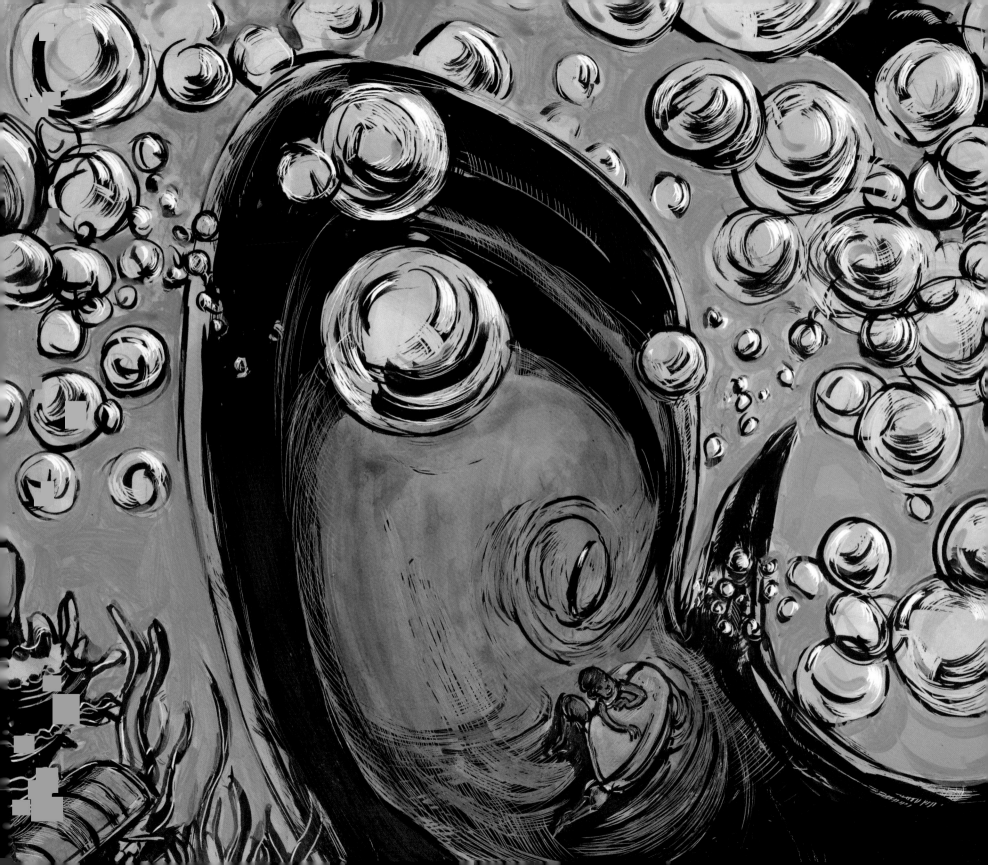

Peggony-Po grabbed tight to Cetus's right fin.
The two of them did a flip-flop tango, with
Peggony-Po taking the lead.

Even though a bag of blubber can be slow,
Cetus had what folks call the weight advantage.
Like a pressing iron flattening a shirtsleeve, Cetus
pinned Peggony-Po, down, down, down to the
very bottom of the sea.

Peggony-Po started to worry that the whale
would mash him into pulp. Then he ribbed Cetus
in his most ticklish spot, right in the pit of his fin.
Cetus couldn't help but let loose a whale's giggle.
He giggled so hard, the whole sea bubbled. At the
same time, he set the boy free. Now it was
Peggony-Po who laughed harder.

Wooden boys don't have to breathe like real boys, so Peggony-Po could stay underwater as long as he pleased. But whales are different. Even whales with determination—and a giggle on their lips—need to come up for air. Cetus raced to the water's surface, and *blew*.

That made a wind so powerful that folks took it for a twister. They prayed for their chickens and fled to their storm cellars until the wind stopped blowing.

Peggony-Po hoisted himself onto Cetus's head. It took Cetus a full minute to figure out how to throw him off. Not only do whales *move* slow, they *think* slow. Peggony-Po gathered up floating strands of seaweed from the ocean floor and braided himself a seaweed harness. He tied himself on and hung tight.

This made Cetus madder than ten whales. He tried to fling off the boy. But Peggony-Po just said, "Hey, whale, the view from here is mighty fine."

Well, Cetus wasn't having it. He spun in circles through the water, trying to shake off Peggony-Po. Finally, Cetus came up with a new plan— to swim the globe and *ride* that kid off his back.

Over the next three days Cetus and Peggony-Po became a traveling spectacle. They sped from oceans to bays, from tropical waters to icy coasts. "What a way to see the world!" Peggony-Po said.

Once, Cetus and Peggony-Po even passed by the *Windstead*.

"*My boy!*" Galleon hollered. Even though this gave Peggony-Po more determination to keep going, he began to wonder if Cetus would *ever* wear out.

Peggony-Po could hear the whale's stomach growling with hunger. Cetus had worked up a whale of an appetite. He finally opened wide and began to eat everything in his path.

The whale's open mouth gave Peggony-Po an idea.

Peggony-Po called out to every ship, port, sailor, and whaler he and Cetus passed. "This whale's hungry! Feed him anything you got!"

Right away somebody flung a broken bullhorn. Next came the roof of a salt shack. Cetus chewed on those shingles like they were the crispiest bacon. When a butter churn splashed down, Cetus savored every bite. Oh, and all those broken barn doors were as tasty as chowder crackers—and much crunchier.

Cetus plunged ahead, chomping on anything that came his way. A potbellied stove. An ironsmith's anvil. An oxcart. Cetus let loose a burp of delight. Finally, all that junk began to slow Cetus down.

Peggony-Po was far from done. "Send this whale some dessert!" he called out. Soon came a leather saddle and somebody's old undies. Cetus flipped to his back to help the food settle.

Swimming upside down confused Cetus. It wasn't long before he crashed hard onto the shore. His body brought down even the biggest trees. And that wasn't all that broke. With his belly so full, Cetus busted his gut!

He thumped his tail once and took a final gasp of air. He died a happy whale, stuffed to his gills.

At first, people thought the rumble made by Cetus's tail hitting the land was some kind of earthquake. Then they saw Cetus belly-up on the shore.

There was no doubt about it: Cetus lay dead as an oarlock. Peggony-Po fetched himself a harmonica and played a proper sailor's farewell.

"You put up a good fight, whale," Peggony-Po said.

Later, with the northern lights showing him the way, Peggony-Po did the backstroke all the way home, dragging Cetus on a tether of seaweed strands, tied to his ankles.

The ship's crew rejoiced. Cetus's flesh made enough lard to last many winters. They boiled his blubber to make casks of a perfume they called Ocean Gold. Galleon carved precious scrimshaw from Cetus's teeth. When the *Windstead* docked, Galleon caught a good price for his wares. He was prosperous beyond measure. And he was richest in his gratitude to his son.

Many nights Peggony-Po and his pa danced a slap-down jig while the *Windstead*'s crew sang the shanty for which the boy had been named. They changed the song's words to fit the times. The tune was the same, though. And so was the joy that went with it!

Oh, he's captured bounty from the sea below,
  Peggony-Po, Peggony-Po!
The boy has brought us peace, oh-ho!
  Peggony-Po, Peggony-Po!
Now we needn't fear the undertow!
  Peggony-Po, where it blows?
Peggony-Po! Peggony-Po! Peggony-Po! Peggony-Po!

"There Blows!"

Whales are the biggest creatures on earth. They have long been the subject of myth and legend. For centuries, sailors feared whales for their mammoth size. They believed that whales could swallow anything in their wake, even whole ships. They also believed that whales were big fish, rather than mammals.

In 1847, whaling was one of the most lucrative industries in the world, with the United States leading the whaling business. Black whalers began working in the early 1700s, when whaling ships that sailed the waters of Africa's west coast and the Caribbean allowed local men on board as crew members. As the slave trade expanded, some black men became fugitives on whale ships, and later proved themselves to be valuable sailors. Whaling was one of the few American industries of the eighteenth and nineteenth centuries that fostered equality. A ship's captain sought out the strongest men, those who could endure months at sea and could master the skill of harpooning a whale. Black sailors and white sailors worked side by side on whaling ships. Among whalers there was little room for prejudice. Back then, the sea was known as an "equalizer of men."

GLOSSARY

Cetus All whales are *cetaceans*, a word derived from the Latin word *cetus*, which means "whale."

First mate The sailor second in command to the ship's captain.

Lookout mast A tall pole used to support the sails of a ship, upon which sailors perch to get a long view of the sea.

Shanty A shanty (also spelled *chantey* or *chanty*) was a work song sung by sailors. Sea shanties were one of the key aspects of marine life that were originated by black sailors; many were based on the rhythms of slave spirituals.

"There blows!" When a sailor spotted a whale, he let others know by shouting "There blows!" Fellow sailors often responded by calling out the inquiry, "Where blows?" "There *she* blows!" is an improper use of the phrase.

FOR FURTHER READING

McKissack, Patricia C., and Frederick L. *Black Hands, White Sails: The Story of African American Whalers*. New York: Scholastic Press, 1999.